Little Worlds of Water

AN EARLY READER

Little Worlds of Water

AN EARLY READER

MARY T KINCAID

ReadersMagnet, LLC

Little Worlds of Water
Copyright © 2022 by Mary Kincaid

Published in the United States of America
ISBN   Paperback: 978-1-959165-84-2
ISBN   eBook: 978-1-959165-85-9

All rights reserved. No part of this publication may be reproduced, stored in a retrieval system or transmitted in any way by any means, electronic, mechanical, photocopy, recording or otherwise without the prior permission of the author except as provided by USA copyright law.

The opinions expressed by the author are not necessarily those of ReadersMagnet, LLC.

ReadersMagnet, LLC
10620 Treena Street, Suite 400 | San Diego, California, 92131 USA
1.619. 354. 2643 | www.readersmagnet.com

Book design copyright © 2022 by ReadersMagnet, LLC. All rights reserved.

Cover design by Ericka Obando
Interior design by Dorothy Lee

CHAPTER ONE

It was my first day of summer vacation. I put my feet on the floor and breathed in freedom.

"Mason, Mason…" a voice called. "It's Dubber up here on the shelf."

I looked up to see the little grey whirl walking along the edge of my entertainment center. His buddies trailed behind him. They marched toward the computer. They turned toward me small but passionate.

"Play with us!" Dubber shouted.

"No," I said. "Shhhhhhhhh." I tried to shush them.

"Mason, you gotta play with us! It's summer…no school," Dubber said. "It's early we have all day."

"Keep your voices down. I just had my last appointment with Mr. Crumpini, the school therapist, because my mom heard voices in my room. I can't stay in my room all summer and play with you."

"Why not?" Raddit asked. "We want to play games with you and Angela."

The beings marched along the shelf where my computer sat dark. Their blond hair waved, antennas for their universe.

"We want to play. You've gotten rid of the fears of my father, Dunwartis, and the rest of the clan. The children no longer hunt us. It's okay if we play," Dubber said.

"It's not okay. I'm the only one who can see you. The children think I made you up. I told the story of your Punwee races because I wanted the kids to stop hunting you. I let them think I imagined you. I'm going to do regular stuff with other kids this summer. I want to be normal. I gotta go outside. My dad, the Commander's orders… 'Leave your room'."

Grabbing my shorts with cargo pockets. I stowed my music electronics, and left them stomping.

In the kitchen, my mother was washing the dishes from Dad's breakfast. She stopped and ran her damp hands through my dark curly hair kissing the top of my head. I grabbed a bowl of cereal keeping my thoughts to myself, and moved to the dining room table.

It's so hard to move. Everything is so different here in Blytheville, Illinois. This is the first time I've had to make friends on my own. The friends I left in San Diego were surf buddies. We met on the beach, and we went to the same school, same surfing lessons, and spent our time riding the waves. No waves here. No beach either. The sandy strip at the pond is not my perfect Coronado Beach in San Diego. How was I to know the little beings that I see are not seen by everyone.

My mother came out of the kitchen with her coffee and sat beside me. She slowly sipped.

"Are you making plans for summer? Hard to believe… you're now my fifth grader. What are you going to do with your freedom?"

"Awww, mom, Angela is going to help me make some new friends." We shared the silence until I finished eating.

"Going to the park to meet Angela."

I sat on the strip of sand and leaned against my favorite rock. As I looked at the water that used to be my kingdom I wondered about summer plans.

A voice sang from above the culvert and interrupted my thoughts. Angela. The sunlight made her blond head look crowned. I waved. She barreled down the path in her jean shorts and tee shirt and waving a flyer. "Look, boats at the community center. Then racing. I'm going to ask Ted, Stanley, too. A neighborhood boat racing team, want in?"

"Fun. Don't forget you promised to help me. Work on my image. Make new friends," I said.

"Boat racing'll make you normal. We'll say you're imaginative. Racing boats is real." I took the flyer.

"I've already seen the Punwees this morning. Dubber pitched a fit when I wouldn't stay in my room and play. Wait 'til they find out you won't be there either."

"They just don't get it, we can't play video games all the time," Angela said.

"They don't. They don't want to listen to us, either."

More footsteps from above, Ted and Stanley walked down from the bridge to the beach. Stanley, his sandy hair streaked by the sun, also, waved a sheet of paper. Ted's gangly walk moved in rhythm to music I couldn't hear. His bright red hair reflected the light. We watched them come toward us.

"How do I win these guys? Do you know what they think about me?"

"Doesn't matter. We're going to make them your friends," Angela said.

"Angela and Mason, the entertainer," Stanley said. "Let's play baseball," Stanley shoved his flyer at me. Let's form a neighborhood team. We can practice on the old diamond here. Even Angela can play with us," he chattered on. He pointed to the field about half a block from the pond's edge.

Angela stood up and put her hands on her hips. "I play ball better than any of you. You'd be lucky to have me at first base," she taunted. "My dad's a coach."

Alarmed, he saw Angela's anger.

"Well, maybe your dad'll give us some pointers. We could use a coach," Stanley said.

"Will you build a boat with me and Mason? We'll have boat races. You can't play baseball all day."

"Don't know…boat…hummmmm, playing ball all day." Stanley thought a minute revealing his game face. "If you play baseball with me, Angela. I'll build boats with you."

"Stanley, I don't know how to play baseball. Are you going to teach me? Maybe I'm no good," I said.

"Teaching Mason baseball will my goal," Angela said.

"My brothers and I will play with you, too. Come to my house, today, we'll get started," he said.

CHAPTER TWO

I wanted lunch. Angela and Ted walked home with me. Stanley went the other way.

I opened the screen door and said to my mother.

"It's baseball and small boats." I laid the info sheets on the kitchen counter. "Angela wants to race miniature boats. Stanley wants to play baseball. I've never played baseball, but boat building is at the community center."

My mom stood at the counter fixing peanut butter and banana sandwiches for us. I reached around, hugged her, and snagged a piece of banana.

"Excellent, Mason."

"You bet. Does Dad know baseball? He taught me surfin'."

"We'll ask him, I think the squadrons on base play."

"I hope he has time." I was rooting through the crisper drawer, hoping an apple was hiding out.

"Do any of your friends play baseball? Have you asked them?"

"Stanley and his brothers play. I'm going to his house after lunch."

"Mason, you must clean in your room," Mom began. I stood still and waited. She looked me in the eye, willing the dreaded stare of doom into my eyes.

"I found your computer on. You know you're not to play games when you first get up in the morning? What's gotten into you? Are you disobeying your Dad?"

"No mam," I said and dropped my eyes to study my shoes.

"You're going to have to do a better job of dusting and vacuuming because I found too many dust bunnies on your shelves. Big ones that looked like they'd been there for awhile," Mom said.

"Yes, mam. I'll take care of it. Off to Stanley's now."

I walked the two blocks to Stanley's neighborhood. The elm trees on his street don't give off the pungent odor of the black walnut tree in my yard. His street was busy. Younger children built blanket forts, celebrating their freedom. Two figures played catch on the grass in Stanley's front yard. Mike and George, Stanley's brothers, watched me walk up. Mike yelled, "Stan, your imaginative friend is here, the little people guy."

"Coming," Stanley called from inside. He bustled through the front door lugging a black bag that dragged along the ground.

"Don't forget, I'm a beginner," I said. I searched Stanley's face hoping that I didn't see a smile.

Stanley smirked. "My brothers said they'll help me teach you baseball. You forget about little people. Check this bag for a glove. We have plenty. If you're right-handed, you want a glove for your left hand."

He dropped the equipment bag on the porch floor. I rummaged, and pulled out three gloves. There was a black leather one for the left hand, a tan one for the right hand, and a brown one shaped like a cup.

"That brown one's a catcher's mitt," Stanley said. He picked the glove up and put it back in the bag. "You won't use it unless you're a phenom."

"Don't want to be a catcher," I said. "Pretty sure I'm not a phenom."

I put the black leather one on my left hand and studied it, turning it around looking at all angles. Its odor was like the bottom of my closet full of old shoes. Maybe I could do something with this one.

"That's a good one. I bet your Dad'll know how to tighten it up for your hand," he said. He nodded his head. "Take that one with you and see if he can make it fit. Let's play catch. Can you throw a baseball?"

"Don't know." The glove felt clunky on my left hand. I moved to where Stanley indicated. My stomach tightened.

"Watch me," he instructed. "Just use your shoulder and your arm, point where you want the ball to go. To catch, step in front of the ball with the pocket of your glove open. When the ball hits it, close your glove fast. That's all there is to it."

"It sounds easy." I said. I saw Stanley release the ball and stepped in front of it. The ball hit the pocket of my glove and bounced onto the ground. I groaned and bent over to get it.

"So much for easy." I picked up the ball, used my arm and shoulder to throw it back. I threw it just over Stanley's head. He jumped up, missed it, and then went to get it.

I watched him. My tight stomach ached.

"If you practice, you'll be good. Awesome as that story you told at the end of school," Stanley said. "We'll work on batting later."

We threw the ball to each other. My throws were over his head or short on distance. Discouraged I headed home, baseball was going to be work. I wanted to fit in. I willed myself to practice, and to like baseball.

At supper we talked ball. Dad announced he would help me catch and bat. After I did the dishes, he took the glove and re-laced it to fit my hand. I started wearing it in my spare time so I could get used to it. He searched the garage and found his old glove and bat.

"Hold your left shoulder up and bring the ball down in front of you so you can swing your arm in a high arc. Like this." Dad showed me more basics. We practiced catching until it was time to go in.

I wanted to believe I was getting better.

"Play with us." The demand came from the top shelf that evening while I looked for a video about the infield.

"Can't. Learning baseball, sorry. Are you leaving the computer on when I'm not here? My mom came and found it on. She thinks I'm playing video games in the morning."

"Well, she came into your room. She didn't see us. We stood very still and waited until she left. She turned the computer off. Is that what you're talking about?" Dubber said.

"Yes…she wants my room to be cleaner. No dust bunnies…she can see you but she doesn't know what you are. She thinks I'm not doing my job of dusting or vacuuming." I waved my arm toward the shelf where he was standing. "You can't be seen in here playing video games." I whispered. There was silence as they slinked off the shelf and under my bed.

I watched baseball videos on a sports channel until I fell asleep. Baseball is complicated.

We met on the old baseball diamond in the park most mornings.

Afternoons, when Angela wasn't playing a softball game, she helped me practice. I was eating and sleeping baseball.

"Hold your glove in front of you, like this. Breathe," Angela demonstrated. I'd never be as good a player as Angela. This is the second thing she's better at. She can beat me at video games, too. It didn't matter to me. Losing to Angela was a high like riding the big waves. The other kids noticed I wasn't catching on. Stanley worked harder to teach me. He came to my house whenever he could and we practiced. It was embarrassing.

"I don't want to be chosen last. I want to fit into the middle of the kids. Don't even have to be a star, just passible," I confessed to Angela. I wiped the sweat from my forehead with the San Diego Dolphin's hat dad gave me. I know my black curls sprung up every time I took it off, nothing discouraged them. I beat the crown and rolled the brim getting the right hat attitude. I slept with it rolled up between my headboard and my mattress shaping it into something I treasured. I hoped that I looked like a ball player. Didn't feel like one.

"Our team needs to be bigger," Stanley announced. He handed flyers to each one of us. "I want you to pass these out to everyone you can think of who might be a baseball player. I'm going to knock on every door from here to my house and see if anyone plays baseball. You guys do the same."

Angela and I walked home trying to think of players without luck, "I don't know that many kids," I admitted. "I hope that Stanley can find more so he can have his team."

"I'm going to ask my softball team," Angela said.

CHAPTER THREE

The four of us, Angela, Ted, Stanley and I, wandered into the brick Community Center after walking six blocks. Down the dim corridor we found a room of steel shelves containing different brown bottles that smelled chemical, like glue. Along the wall sat rows of small colored jars. Boats and model airplanes waving from the ceiling gave the room movement. The utility gray walls slowed the vibrations, but didn't stop them. A young man, with Andy on his nametag, approached us. He consulted his clipboard. "Boat building and racing?" he asked.

"Yes."

"Stanley, Mason, Ted, and Angela?"

We nodded.

"I'm Andy, and I teach miniature boat building. I'll show you where to sit." We followed him to one of the back corners where bags of supplies decorated a table. "Just have a seat and we'll wait on the others." He studied his clipboard, chewing on his pencil.

We sat down and looked at the six kits on the table in front of us. Each one had four pieces of wood, paint jars, a brush, some waterproof paste, some stencils, and some decals. There were instruction sheets included. A notebook with pictures and examples sat open on the table.

"I've never built anything, have you?" I asked them.

"It'll be fun, you'll like it," Angela offered. "I've built things from kits. We have everything we need in front of us."

"Look at all the wooden pieces. Wonder what the trick to it'll be?" Stanley said. "I made a clay dish at nursery school with my handprint in it, does that count?"

"Something else, I probably can't do," Ted said. He poked at his kit with his fingers as if it was something dangerous. "I'm going to build the easiest one."

We sat our kits in front of us, and waited for Andy. Ted fiddled with his bag string. Angela studied the various shapes. She turned the pieces over, fingered the decals, and counted the paint jars. Stanley bounced his left leg like a racer lined up for a dash. I waited. I'd never attended a community craft class. When two more kids, Sam and Ann, came in, the class started. They made six in the class. They built boats before and greeted Andy as an old friend.

Andy talked about boat designs. He described hull shapes that affect speed. He gave handouts of finished model boats. He encouraged us to pick out a boat type and work to shape the front of our boat. Angela picked a racing hull. Her competitive spirit showed as she studied the design.

As I looked through the design manual, a little idea struck me. I just studied the pictures and didn't say a word to anyone about it. I knew where I could go for reference. *What if?*

Stanley's enthusiasm built as he studied the designs. "I'm going to dazzle my brothers with my boat."

"I want to engineer the best boat," Sam said. He pulled out his draft paper and began to draw. He was dark skinned with black hair and eyes. His precise English and accent reminded me of a faraway place. "My father will help me," he said. I watched him and wondered if his design could beat Angela's.

Stanley shoved me with his knee and pointed to the graph paper. "Where's yours?" I shrugged. I looked into my bag and there it was. "Here." I pulled it out showing Stanley.

"You have an idea?" Stanley asked.

"I do but it is a secret. Will show you later." I moved the notebook over so we could share it and we studied the designs.

Ann quietly assembled her hull, shaping and sanding it until she was satisfied. She didn't have much to say. Her brown eyes hid behind her dark hair and her glasses.

Ted didn't say much. He studied his pieces and watched each of us. He spent a long time looking at the notebook of boat designs.

The next morning I took my graph paper to the garage and studied my surf board to see what parts I could use in my boat project. I sketched and measured it. Dad could check my math so I could bring it down to scale for my design. I drew the fins that were on the bottom back of the board maybe I could use them to shape the back of my boat. Being in the garage looking at my old equipment made me happy as I worked. That design work became my boat design basics. I adapted, and improvised. I sanded, carved until the hull cut through the water. I tested it in the sink that stood in the back corner of the room.

"Your concept is very interesting," Andy said. "Where did you get your idea?"

"From my surfboard," I said. "It was fast. I miss riding the waves on it."

"I bet, no surf in Blytheville. But we can sail here on the lakes, if you want to consider sailing."

"Thanks."

Andy showed us the math for each one of our hull designs, but it was hard for me to follow.

Ann quietly built her boat like a pro. She modified another racing design and worked while four of us laughed and joked. Sam applied himself without interacting with the rest of us, and he ignored Ann. She finished and painted her boat bright pink, explaining to Angela that it was a festival boat.

I left the sides of my design shallow. It had a long lean look. I rounded the front hull and gave the bottom a concave shape. My hull was white with a red racing stripe, and it floated high in the sink of water.

When all of the boats lined up for Andy's final inspection, Ann and Sam laughed at my design.

"Boats are low in the water," Sam said. Ann giggled with him as she pointed at mine.

"It rides a little high," Ann said.

"Never mind them," Angela said. "They don't know anymore than we do."

"Am I fitting in?" I whispered to her. From their expressions, I had my doubts. Angela rolled her eyes and turned her face away.

Andy drew our attention.

"Who will win the racing contest?" Andy asked as he surveyed the designs.

"I want mine to float," I said.

"I want to win," Angela said. She held her boat as if she had already won the trophy.

"I want to finish," Ted said.

"Can't wait to show my brothers," Stanley said. "See you at practice."

Our last Saturday at the community center, Stanley, Ted, Angela and I walked to the ball field. The morning smelled of fresh mowing, and roses. The backstop stood in one corner of the park barely visible from the street. Stanley and his brothers did the weed eating, down the lines, and around the small metal bleachers. The park division did the mowing. Our practices made paths down the base lines, and the old boards we used as bases sat where we left them. This was the day we would meet the players he contacted with his flyers.

"I hope they show up," Stanley said.

"I know that some of my softball team are coming. As long as there are no game conflicts, they'll play," Angela said.

"Great, a whole infield. Awesome!" Stanley's face glowed with anticipation as he punched the pocket of his glove.

Six players milled around the backstop waiting. Stanley hurried over to take their names and get their positions. There were Jae and Mi, Korean twins who played outfield. Ali was a catcher. Melody played shortstop, and Amy played second base. Meredith played third base. Angela played first base, and Stanley liked to pitch.

"Becka, will rotate on our bench. She'll keep our team from looking lame," Stanley said. He waved his notebook and pencil around.

When Ted saw the other players, he took his glove and walked home. Stanley and I went after him.

"I hate losing. Not being good at things, I don't like baseball. I don't want to play on a team with girls on it. I hate watching Angela be better," Ted groused. "It's awful losing to a girl. No, thanks." He harrumphed off and started down the street toward his house. We watched him go. Stanley shrugged.

"Let's get in some practice." Stanley picked up his glove and ball and headed to the pitcher's mound.

"Mason look up!" Angela called. I didn't get my glove up fast enough and looked up just in time to see the ball bring stars to my right eye. I lay on the ground trying to get my head to stop spinning when Angela's face became clearly outlined.

"Come on, I'll walk you home," Angela said. "Practice called for the day."

"Not sure I'm good at baseball," I said to Mom as I lay on the sofa with a bag of frozen peas on my eye.

Drills led by the softball girls filled the next couple of days. The new recruits were outstanding players. I never developed the sixth sense I saw in the infield girls about where the ball was going next. They just knew where the play was going to happen, Stanley did too. My ball handling still suffered. I recognized my limits. The new arrivals created the Second Street Neighborhood Team.

"Mason, watch out!" Stanley called. Just then my feet tangled. I bobbled to the right and the ball dropped to the left. I heard Stanley groan even though he thought he was being quiet.

The next afternoon I was in left field surrounded by butterflies. I missed catches because I watched them flit around the blooming park shrubs. *Maybe baseball was not going to be my sport?*

Finally Stanley came to me. "I think I have a position for you. Would you be the manager? You'd keep track of our equipment and stuff. I'll check with the other teams and get a game lineup. It would be a big help."

"Yes, I'll manage. I want to be part of the team," I said. Finally I saw a way out of this embarrassing position.

"Can I be normal if I don't play baseball?" I asked Angela as we walked home.

"You'll be normal. It's okay if you don't have baseball skills, I'm sure we can find other things you can do."

I set the supper table and waited for my family to join me.

"Dad, I'm never going to be good at baseball. I hope that's okay," I said. He'd finished his pie and rested his coffee cup on its saucer. He turned and looked at me.

"I'm proud of you, no matter what," he said. He smiled at me. "I'm glad that you tried it."

"Surfing, was my thing," I said.

"Other things, too. You'll find other things," Dad said.

"Wish I could be good at everything."

"When I was a boy, I tried many things to discover what I was good at. Trying things is what being a boy is all about. Maybe baseball isn't your thing. What would you like to try next? I don't expect you to be good at everything, just want you to get out and try."

"Okay, I'll think about what I want to do next," I said.

"That's the spirit," Dad said.

"The boat races for the Fourth of July will be next week," I said. I waded out into the pond and put my little white and red design in the water. Angela's red racer shot past mine as it slid downstream toward the spillway.

"Ha! My boat is fast," Angela said. She stood with her hands raised in victory as she watched it slide through the water.

"Hurry, it's going over the edge," I said. She rushed past me to catch her boat.

Among the rocks that cascaded down from the bridge a silver flash stood watching. I glimpsed the sparkle as the sun reflected but maybe I was mistaken.

CHAPTER FOUR

"Mason and I can't spend all summer playing video games with you," Angela said to Dubber. She couldn't see him but she did hear him.

"We want to play with you," he said. His voice pleaded with her. "It's summer and everyone needs to be outside playing another game." Angela continued to listen to his arguments but wasn't persuaded.

"How are we going to get outside and play," Dubber asked.

"Good question. Can you be outside if it is not an official race day?" I turned to Angela and lifted my shoulders. "I don't know what the rules are? Even as Presage, the person who speaks for Punwees to humans, I've never been told a set of rules."

"We've never been outside. We're Dust Bunny Punwees. We live under your bed and along the baseboards," Dubber said. "Exploring might be a good thing." His voice was thoughtful as he stood next to his buddies.

Just then Frisbee, my cat, came into my room and hopped upon the bed. Angela and I picked up our equipment and left to practice.

Breakfast was usually quiet at my house. Eating my cereal after my dad left for work didn't involve much suspense. I hunched over my bowl as Frisbee came into the room. Dusty lumps clustered across the back of Frisbee's neck. What were they? Then I realized! Three Punwees perched on Frisbee just like the tourists I saw riding a camel on the Nat Geo Special I watched with my dad.

My mom was at the sink. I didn't turn around for fear my expression would alarm her. Frisbee laid under the table. The Punwees looked around the kitchen. I don't know if they'd ever been this far from my room. I waited holding my breath.

"Mason, look at the dust ring around Frisbee's neck. You are going to go upstairs and do something about your room. It's not clean or Frisbee wouldn't be so dusty."

The Punwees sat very still.

"I'll take care of it, Mom."

"Go, do it now. Take the vacuum cleaner and run it in your room after you've dusted."

I got up from the table and walked to the hall closet to get the vacuum. Frisbee followed me up the stairs, the Punwee's still clinging to his neck.

"What do you think you are doing?" I asked quietly when we arrived in my room. "Are you leaving my room now? What's gotten into you?"

"Angela said we should have outside games and we are going to find a game," Dubber said. His little shoulders squared in defiance.

"How did you get Frisbee to give you a ride?"

"We asked him. He thought it was a good idea, he wants to get out, too," Dubber said. "This was our first ride, but I look forward to what I can see."

"I don't feel good about this," I said. I plugged in the vacuum cleaner since I finished my dusting.

"Then play with us in your room," Dubber said.

I turned on the vacuum.

I heard Spooky, Angela's dog, barking furiously early next morning when I woke up and found Frisbee nowhere in sight. I raced downstairs to see why the little mop of a dog was so loud. Angela never let him out of his yard- why would he sound so close?

Spooky stood at the base of the walnut tree in our yard leaping, growling, twelve pounds of fury, a racing blur circling. High in the crook by the branch not far from my bedroom window sat Frisbee. Three small lumps of dust clung to his neck.

I stopped and scooped up Spooky.

"I'll take you home," I said. I turned and walked across the street to Angela's. A sleepy eyed Angela opened the door in her pajamas.

"I was dressing so I could hunt for him. I heard him barking but didn't know where he was."

"He treed Frisbee. I'm going to coax the cat down."

As Angela closed the door, I turned and saw Frisbee navigating his descent from the tree. I rushed over and picked him up. The Punwees still clung to his neck fur.

"We slipped through the door when your dad left for work. The world is very bright first thing in the morning. What was that loud white fuzzy thing that chased Frisbee?"

"That was Spooky, Angela's dog."

"Cat very fast, good climber," Dubber said. "We held on tight."

I took Frisbee inside. He slipped unseen past my mother rinsing dishes at the sink, and scurried up the stairs to my room with his riders. I looked high in the walnut tree, and saw nestled in a tree limb fork, tiny brown figures, Tolemar, the Miniscule, standing and watching the cat, and the dog.

"Looks like trouble to me," Tolemar said. Ives and Winsor, his companions, nodded their heads in agreement. "We never venture out of our clan living area. Wonder what this is all about?" The three of them stood there in silence staring after Mason and the cat.

Being manager was safer than being in the outfield. I lugged our equipment bag and bottles of water. Stanley's brothers drove us to other neighborhoods when we had an away game.

"You are a great manager!" Stanley said to me, taking a sip from his bottle of water.

"Great to be part of the team," I said. Angela winked at me and gave me thumbs up sign.

Our uniform was a tee shirt and a cap in bright green. The shirt had Second Street Neighborhood across the back in navy blue. The bright green cap had a dark blue bill.

Ali called to us, "Get those hats in shape. We don't want to look like the new kids."

I said, "Yeh, will give it special attention."

They were a great bunch of fourth, fifth, and sixth graders. Jae and Mi would be in my fifth grade class next fall.

CHAPTER FIVE

I sat at the base of the stream runoff before ball practice and watched the pale blue translucent flashes march down from the rocks above me. A dropping splash of water ran through the park beginning at the rocky culvert by the entrance gates. From among the rocks lining the sides of moving water a cluster sparkled, moved, and relocated where the water gathered together and formed the park pond. Their pale iridescent blue skin blended into the water and rocks like fish scales and hid them in plain sight.

"Start looking at the oak leaves," the leader instructed.

"Seamoss, Seamoss, where do we look?" a tiny voice called.

Seamoss instructed, "I'm leading you to the oak leaf field now, follow me." The shiny beings flashed up the hill and searched among the leaves on the ground.

Seamoss said, "Don't stop now and eat acorns. Come back later and do that. Now we are looking for leaves."

Seamoss dragged a leaf into the circle of students.

"Gather round. Here are the parts of the leaf you need to judge. Is the front pointed? Will it cut through the water swiftly? Look at the center vein," he pointed to the line down the middle of the leaf. "Need deep indentations along this main line for swirling in the pools of rapids." The students gathered closer. "Finally the leaf stem…will it help you to steer the gaps between the hazards? Everyone try to find a leaf."

Flashes moved out. Then leaves swirled and moved toward Seamoss.

Seamoss arranged his students by size. The students lined up with their leaves, one placed on each side of them. He stood and studied his work as they lined up.

I watched the cluster of Punwees move to the water reeds along the bank pulling their leaves with them.

"Every skilled deluger must learn how to craft reed ropes. It is for their safety and protection. The steering handles must allow riders to steer their leaves."

Pipper, a student, spoke up, "I want to learn how to stand up and spin in the air as I fly through the water!"

Seamoss said, "When I've decided who your partner will be, then we'll talk about spinning. You haven't been paired yet. You're getting ahead of yourself."

They gathered parts of the reeds and brought them to the bank. As they worked the strings, weaving them and tying them, I could see lengths of material forming.

"Every rider has to depend on his ropes for safety," Seamoss said as he moved from pair to pair inspecting and reinforcing their materials. "You need handles and guide lengths."

Finally I spoke, "Are you Punwees?"

They scattered. I watched them hide among the waterweeds and the oak leaves.

"You can see us?" Seamoss asked.

"I can hear you, too," I answered.

Seamoss said, "No one has ever seen us before."

"I'm your Presage. But I've only met the Dust Bunny Clan, and the Walnut Clan. I heard that Punwees are everywhere, but you are the first ones I've seen in water."

"We are everywhere. We are the Leaf Riders. These little ones are just learning how to get ready for their partners and rides. They are in training. I'm their instructor," Seamoss said.

I couldn't wait to return to the beach and study the Leaf Riders. I missed surfing so much and I wanted to learn about their rides. Many mornings I lay on the beach and watched for Water Punwees. Finally, a pair of riders moved their leaf to their discharge point. I didn't tell anyone about them. I didn't want to make the same mistake I made when I first moved here by talking about the tiny beings. *I wish I could do that, the ride looks amazing.*

LITTLE WORLDS OF WATER

As I watched, I listened. I could make out the words. The leaves stopped on a small patch of gravel. They slid from the bank into the water. The oak leaf navigated the dropping rapids. On the leaf, tiny beings sparkled like sequins on my mom's sweater. I focused on two tiny riders shifting their weight driving the leaf around the rocky hazards. The leaf careened down toward me picking up speed. As they swept past me, they moved onto the centerline of the leaf and slowed their ride by leaning back until they coasted to the middle of the pond. The front rider lay down on his stomach and paddled with his arms toward shore. The iridescent blue-gray of the riders blended into the water, and I lost sight of them for a minute.

More voices tinkled in the breeze.

"Whoa, this is so rad," Dubber said.

"Yeah, great…"Fluw said.

"Totally," Raddit added. "Look at everything!"

I searched for the voices. Frisbee, my gray tabby cat, came walking along the sand. I'd never seen Frisbee this far from our yard. Immediately I knew why. Gray whorls attached to his neck between his ears: Dubber, Raddit, and Fluw.

"Why are you at the park…this far from home? What are you up to? Does your dad know you can get this far?"

His dad, Dunwartis, the Dust Bunny Clan leader, was pretty strict about his son following the Punwee Clan rules.

"Summer is for parks. No reason to stay in your room, looking for our new game," Dubber said. He ignored my other questions and continued. "We wanted to see where other clans live. The only time we're at the park is for the races." He gestured spreading his arms. "There are interesting things in this park: water, trees, things we don't have in your room."

Frisbee lay beside me, and the Punwees dropped down onto the sand.

"This water and sand is amazing. I want to learn how to move in the water," Dubber said. He swirled the sand with his foot.

"Can't you swim already?" I asked.

"No. We don't do everything. I'll get one of the Water Clan Punwees to show me. I'll teach them how to play video games. I'll make some new friends," Dubber said. Raddit and Fluw shook their heads in agreement. "I know one or two of them. Here comes some now." Dubber turned to face the water and watched another the leaf dropping down the slope.

The second leaf entered the currents. We saw them coast into the middle of the pond.

"Come, introduce yourselves," Dubber called, waving them over.

The Riders acknowledged him, and moved toward the beach where the Punwees stood. I sat and watched. Their translucent silver hair reflected the sunlight.

The riders waded to the beach and pulled their leaf. The other one turned and said to Dubber, "Hi, I'm Seamoss of the Leaf Riders, one of the Culvert Clans. Can you swim? What clan are you from?"

"We are from the Dust Bunny Clan. We live under the furniture in the Presage's room. We've learned to play video games and we'll teach you. Mason, our Presage, will help us." Dubber waved in my direction and Seamoss nodded.

"My name is Dubber. That leaf ride looks like so much fun. Will you show us how to do it? We have things we can teach you," Dubber said.

"I met the Presage when I was teaching," he said. He turned facing me as I sat there. "What's a Presage?" he asked.

"It's someone who talks to the human beings for you. Helping you when you have problems with them," I said.

"We don't have problems. We've never been seen. You're the first," a voice said.

"This leaf belongs to the team of Seamoss-Shonar. We are currently the champions, but that may change after the clan's next race."

The second leaf rider spoke to Dubber and his crew.

"My name is Shonar. Leaf riding is dangerous, not everyone should do it," he said.

I listened. My expertise was the outside world, communicating for the Punwees with humans. This was one clan talking to another. Something I knew nothing about.

The five of them sat down on the beach and chatted. Then the leaf riders picked up their leaf and said, 'Good-by.'

Dubber, Reddit and Fluw called Frisbee from the shade, and climbed onto his neck.

"We'll introduce you to our transport, Frisbee, next time," Dubber said. Shonar and Seamoss waved and climbed up the path pulling their leaves.

The next morning I met the other championship team of leaf riders as they practiced for the upcoming competition.

"I'm Danu, and, my partner is Phylla. The other team is Seamoss and Shonar. Can you see us?" she asked.

"Yes, I can see you. You're beautiful, all of you," I said. Their sparkle still dazzled me.

"You may watch our ride. We have to start now before the park gets too busy," Danu said. "Children come to float trash from the bridge. We are practicing for the races."

I sat as the two active deluging teams climbed the rocks so they could ride.

"I've pinned my hair up so there won't be a drag to slow me down, what are you going to do with the bush that's on your head, Seamoss," called Danu, the Darling. "Its wind resistance is like a wall." She stooped over her leaf, checking her woven rope knots waiting for her partner Phylla, the Pleasant. Phylla came running breathless smiling. She pursed her lips making kissing sounds to the other delugers on the bank.

"Don't be hurling trash kisses up to us," Seamoss yelled, shaking his fist.

"Taunts are part of the ride, Presage, we get points for taunts," Danu shouted. Their ceremony transfixed me.

She grabbed the back end of her leaf looking briefly at her handle knots. "Let's go," she shouted.

They slid their leaf into the water and lay down on opposite sides of it. They began to paddle to the middle of the creek where the current was the strongest. Then their ride began. As the leaf engaged the current, they both stood up and waved to the other team on the bank. "See you in the basin," they called over their shoulders. The current carried them along swiftly until they entered the first hazard. Seamoss and Shonar stood beside me next to their leaf.

"I'll explain the course to you, Presage. First hazard we call the death spiral because the swirl of water traps riders and throws them onto the banks," he began. "Many beginning riders are thrown onto the rocky banks where they are taunted and shamed by anyone watching. "Phylla and Danu are good at clearing the death spiral. They will shift their positions to the back of the leaf and come out of the first turn jumping clear of the swirling water."

I watched them reenter the current in the middle of the stream. "That's amazing," I said.

"Three Elders up next," yelled Danu, "get ready."

"The Three Elders are two boulders on the right side of the stream and one on the left placed so that they form a triangle. This triangle, if not navigated on the left side of the current, traps leaves in a pool and can throw the riders against the rocks to cause injuries," Seamoss said.

I watched.

"Okay…ready, shift," called Phylla. They moved to the right side of the leaf and pulled on their handles almost sliding their leaf onto its side. They knifed through the triangle's gap. As soon as they cleared the boulders, they moved to the center and set the leaf down flat in the water, moving along once again.

"Killer Falls coming up," shouted Danu.

"What's Killer Falls?" I asked Seamoss.

"Killer Falls is a three rock drop as the water descends rapidly downstream. The current becomes faster as the water narrows forcing a smaller space with a longer drop. Many experienced riders are hurt at Killer Falls," Seamoss said.

The Riders readied themselves extending their rope handles and moving into position in the center toward the back of the leaf. They squatted down and their leaf sailed up into the air. Up, up, up, up, soaring over the falls and finally coming down with a splash just after the hazard. The riders held still as the leaf landed. They immediately moved to the opposite edge so they could paddle into the current and away from the opposing rocks.

"On my signal," ordered Danu, "now!" They both began to paddle on their sides of the leaf. The leaf stayed in the center of the current away from the boulders. The riders continued to paddle until they were clear. They then stood up and sailed into the basin triumphantly. I sat and waited for them to come ashore.

"Way to go," shouted the Riders on the bank as the Punwee Riders stood up in their victory salute.

"I've never seen anything like that," I said. "What a beautiful ride! I use to do something like leaf riding, but I don't now cause I'm too far from the ocean surf. It wasn't exactly like your ride, but close. It was called surfing, but it was done on a wooden board in a bigger body of water."

"Was your board better than a leaf," Danu asked. "Make a drawing in the sand so we can see it."

I picked up a stick and drew a rough outline of a surfboard.

"It was pointed in the front like this, and flatter on the bottom than your leaf." I continued to draw.

Seamoss studied the drawing.

"It is like the leaf, but harder," he said. He walked around looking at his oak leaf and then at the drawing. "Hummmmmmmmm. You used to do leaf riding? Maybe you would help us to build one?"

"Maybe...," I said. "Would the elders and the council approve?"

"Don't know," Seamoss said. "Have to ask 'em. We have to go now, maybe we'll see you again sometime."

"Yes, maybe," I said.

Dubber paced and whirled before standing still as he delivered the news.

"We've been summoned before the council," he said.

"Do you know what they want?" I asked.

"My Dad says they want to discuss riding Frisbee. I never rode a cat before so not sure what the problem is."

The council was a solid wall of disapproval as they stood shoulder to shoulder. Dubber, Raddit, and Fluw stood facing them in front of me. The young Punwees had their backs to me but I could see their stiff shoulders and tight necks. I stood holding my breath the gravity of the situation washing over me. Dunwartis, Dust Bunny Clan leader and Dubber's father, stood with the three teenagers. Tolemar, the Miniscule, stepped forward and began to recite in a sing-song voice.

"The Walnut Clan reported to this body that Punwees were seen in a tree outside their territory riding a furry beast. The Council is concerned about the reports of beast rides, the animal known as cat, by the unauthorized youth of the Dust Bunny Clan. The Dust Bunny clan resides under the bed and along the baseboards of the Presage's room and is not approved for outside adventure. They must answer the following three questions: First, How did they come by the cat for riding? Second, Why did they want to leave their assigned territory? Third, Isn't playing video games enough of a break from tradition for them?"

Dubber stepped forward and cleared his throat. He began to speak in a squeaky voice. "The cat belongs to the Presage. We were afraid of it before we met it, but it is a gentle creature and means no harm. Now that we know how to talk to it, we ask it to take us to places we never dreamed we could go."

Tolemar said, "You talked to the cat? The only clans that have domesticated animals are the bird riders. No one has ever communicated with a beast that is so big and hazardous."

"We want the beast before us. Unless you think he might harm us."

"The beast is kind," Dubber said.

"Can you answer the next charge?" Tolemar asked. Dubber replied, "We want to see other parts of the world, especially the park. The only part of the park we have explored is the place where we hold our Spring Races. We want to see the other parts. To answer the last question…we don't know about the tradition that keeps us from learning new things. What's wrong with learning to play video games? What is wrong with seeing new places?"

Tolemar stared over the petition at the three young Punwees before him. "Tradition has kept us safe for many generations. The proper keeping of it is the work to which we are called. How dare you question its value?" His glare darkened as he completed his speech.

Dubber, Raddit, and Fluw stood with their heads bowed. As an observer, I searched the faces along the wall and did not find a single smile or encouraging expression.

Tolemar stepped forward. "We will wait to meet the beast."

I sat and watched not knowing how I could help.

We returned to meet with the Council the next morning with Frisbee. Frisbee sat and watched while Dubber, Raddit, Fluw, and Dunwartis stood in front of him. I sat outside of the circle while Tolemar approached them.

"Is this the cat?" he asked. He pointed at Frisbee. He held his hand high. Frisbee's size dwarfing him as he stood in the cat's shadow.

Frisbee lowered his nose until it almost brushed against him. Very still, Tolemar stood his ground as the cat breathed on him fluttering his hair, his fist clenched in fear. Finally Tolemar lifted his hand, relaxed it, and stroked Frisbee's nose.

"Presage, is this your cat? I see he is a gentle beast. But the Council will vote on whether leaving home territory is allowed and will give its decision."

With that we were dismissed.

I stretched from the bank as far as I could to put my boat into the current. Angela stood beside me and dropped her boat into the water.

"Look at my Scarlet going around your boat, Striper," she called. She pointed, jumped, and circled her arm and fist. "I will win the race!"

My white and red striped craft slid through the water just behind hers as they swirled into the pond basin. As the summer wore on we spent less time on baseball, we only had one more game scheduled. Second Street Neighborhood baseball team was on the short list for the playoffs, and we might even make it. Stanley's daily pilgrimage to the Community Center kept me updated on our league standing. I hoped for his sake that we might make the first round, but could live with my current baseball experience.

"Practicing our water entry is a good idea." I fetched my craft and moved up the bank.

"I think race entry will be right next to the culvert so let's practice there," Angela said and moved toward the dropping water.

I looked up to see Seamoss glittering in the sun and standing along the rocky bank.

"Hello," I called to him.

"Is this the vessel like the one you rode?" he asked. He pointed to the red and white vessel.

I gestured in agreement.

"I changed the design so it is not exactly like my ride."

Seamoss said, "Put it down so I can study it. What do you call it? I see it is not a leaf."

I set the vessel down beside him. He walked around it looking at all angles. "It is called a boat, I named it Striper.

"What's going on?" Angela asked. She moved closer to me and looked at the craft on the sand. "I'm ready to race again." She held her scarlet vessel in her hand.

"Seamoss, the Leaf Rider, is studying my design," I said.

"Turn it over," he said. I flipped it over so that he could study the underneath side. He ran his hands over the hull caressing the smooth curve of its shape.

"I heard the voice, someone I know?" Angela said as she studied the boat on the sand.

"Very hard. Can't control like leaf, not flexible," he muttered. "Beautiful. Maybe I could try it out in the water to see how it steers? Can I ride in it?"

"Voice belongs to Seamoss, the Leaf Rider. Seamoss meet Angela, my friend," I said. Angela studied where I was pointing.

"Okay," I answered. Seamoss gestured to the boat and moved to his entry point.

"What are you doing? Let's race again," Angela said. "I want to practice my entry. I want to win." She wanted to continue proving her superiority. "Where is your boat going?"

I said to her, "The leaf rider wants to try my racer. Let's see how it rides for him," I said.

She swung her blond braid behind her shoulder and put her hands on her hips. She couldn't see him. She listened and nodded affirmative.

"Bring it up here," Seamoss instructed. He waved from the bank above me, closer to the water. I walked to where he stood.

"This might be dangerous. It's not what you're used to, will you be able to steer it?" I asked.

He shrugged and climbed in. Standing in the middle of the craft, he looked small and fragile. He sparkled against the interior paint.

"Shove me away from the bank, Presage," he said.

I did as he instructed and watched as the boat cut through the current. It rode high because his weight did not add to its stability. Seamoss squatted down and grabbed both sides and began to feel for the current. Swirling water took hold of the boat and threatened to turned it around so that Seamoss faced upstream. He raised the left side of the vessel and leaned onto his right side tipping and steering in the direction of the rushing water. He clutched both sides and looked ahead.

"Are you sure that's safe?" Angela asked. My craft picked up speed. Her look of concern mirrored my own. "He sits so high in the water. The craft is not stable enough for a ride. I don't want him in mine."

Seamoss rushed toward the Death Spiral. He had no handholds so he clutched the sides of the boat. He adapted his usual ride, an oak leaf, with many safety features that helped him steer it in the water. He made hand-ropes for it, which gave him more balance and secured him. I had no modifications in the hull giving safety to little rider. He was moving too fast for me to see his expression. He spider-walked backward never letting go of the sides. Facing forward he reached as far back as he could get without climbing over the back edge. The speed of the current lifted the front of the boat and Seamoss stood up bringing the front hull out of the water and shooting over the foaming Death Spiral. He landed in the current past the circular pool. Angela sighed as she watched the boat move downstream to the pond below.

"That was close." She stared transfixed by the drama before her.

Seamoss crawled up the sides of the boat still holding on to both sides. His crouched stance added a little stability to its center. He looked ahead at the Three Elders. The boulders on each side of the stream presented an imposing obstacle for someone his size. I held my breath. The leaf rider never hesitated as he sliced the water.

As he approached the Three Elders, he moved his feet toward the left and continued to hold onto both sides. He jumped and raised the right side of the boat out of the water, knifing through the narrow opening between the rocks. As he came through he flipped his feet back into the center of the boat and centered himself. Nothing he did slowed the craft as it picked up more speed. His approach to the last hazard came quicker than he anticipated. The surge lifted him high in the air and separated him from the boat. I watched horrified as his sparkling glint hovered over the boat and the water.

"Jump clear," I shouted. He struggled in midair to get his bearings, but sailed along with the boat moving below him. He chose the water below Killer Falls rather than the rocks and finally turned his body and dove in slightly behind the boat. I rushed along the shore searching for the glint of his tiny head coming to the surface. My boat, separated from the Leaf Rider's guidance, clipped on toward the bridge at the far end of the pond, its time in the air not slowing it down or making it change course.

"Is the rider okay? Can you see him?" Angela called. She moved along the sand following the empty boat heading toward the spillway.

Finally, as I was going to enter the water to see if I could find Seamoss, he popped to the surface coughing and sputtering.

"That's a RIDE!" He pumped his fist above the water celebrating. "I WANT ONE!"

"Oh…" Angela cried out as she hustled over to the bridge. She reached down and captured my boat as it was about to go over the falls and crash on the rough rocks stacked below.

"Can't lose my competition. I want to win fair and square," she shouted. She raised the boat in the air. "That was close. I think I heard the rider, is he okay?"

CHAPTER SIX

Lingering along the bank among the reeds, Shonar, Danu and Phylla watched Seamoss in the wooden boat.

"Look. What is that?" asked Danu.

"Don't know," responded Phylla. "How could we get a closer?"

Danu said, "I want to inspect one."

They lurked studying Mason and the boats.

"A new way to ride the current. Don't you think?" asked Shonar.

"Definitely possible," said Danu.

They started home along the rock banks.

"Do you think we could make something like it ourselves?" continued Danu.

"What would we use? Wood? Rocks?" mused Phylla. "What shape would we make ours?"

"Imagine what we could do with a deluging ride that wasn't destroyed at the end? No matter how good they are the leaves don't last and we have to find new ones every day."

Danu said, "What kind of ropes do you need to steer it? What would be the best shape? What materials could we find?"

Shonar said, "We could go faster than we ever imagined. Fly like a cool breeze on a hot day."

Danu said, "Has anyone read in the clan histories about anything like this?"

"No," came the muttered answer.

Danu said, "Let's keep a watch on the basin shore so we can observe this phenomenon."

In the morning along the bank the three delugers sat and waited.

"I can't wait to see something that'll ride faster than our leaves," said Danu.

"Yes, new speed records are awesome to think about," agreed Phylla. "I can already feel the wind on my face."

The punwees studied the boat as it lay on the sand. "The hull made from a solid piece of wood," Shonar said.

Danu said, "How can we do this? We'll have to create the tools we need. We've never done anything like this before."

"The sharpest things we have to work with are stones. But some of them are really sharp," commented Shonar standing on the beach beside the bottom of the boat.

"Where'll we find the material?" Shonar began. "Can we find sticks that we wouldn't have to modify?"

"You need a stick that can be hollowed out for a slight bowl shape like your oak leaf. We need to measure leaves and decide the vessel length and width for ease of handling. We'll have to experiment with the shape of the front to see which one delivers the speed you want."

The three Leaf Riders sat down to think.

Shonar picked up a piece of sharp gravel. "Maybe we match the shape to an oak leaf? Let's study an oak leaf. We know how to navigate it in the water."

"Let's hunt for sticks that wouldn't have to have much modification," Phylla said. "We need a stick that can be hollowed out for a slight bowl shape like our oak leaf. Delugers need to decide the vessel length and width for ease of handling. Danu and I will find the sticks, you develop the tools we need to construct it."

"What about material caught in the current by the bridge?" asked Danu. "I bet we could find something there."

"We've looked and found these two pieces of driftwood," Danu said. They started toward the beach pulling their finds with them.

Shonar collected small sharp pieces of gravel and tested them for sharpness. He gave a tool to each of them.

CHAPTER SEVEN

Stanley was thrilled when The Second Street Neighborhood made the playoffs. The rest of the team ate and slept baseball, but Stanley breathed it. He dusted a place on the shelf in his room for his future championship trophy, even though we were one playoff game away from winning it. He plotted strategy.

"Stop this. You act like we've never won a tournament before. The girls on my softball team are city league champions. You're insulting," Angela said. "Our infield is a precision machine, our outfield has champion arms and eagle eyes. You're making us crazy."

Jae and Mi slapped their ball caps across their thighs, releasing their black manes and shaking them in disapproval. They flashed their dark eyes. Becka put her hands on her hips.

"The outfield is tired of hearing about this," Becka said. The infield girls nodded their agreement.

Ali, the catcher, looked at Stanley and sighed. "My little brother acts just like you when someone takes his teddy bear. He won't stop screaming until he has it back. Stop screaming and let's play ball. I didn't think we would get this far."

"Okay, playoff game is next Tuesday at 2:00 and we are the home team. Everyone ready?" Heads nodded in agreement.

I found Frisbee on the beach during my next pond visit. I couldn't hear the conversation of the Punwee gathering, and didn't have time to stop because I was heading to baseball practice with my wagon full of water and equipment.

The Dust Bunny Punwees stood next to Frisbee while Seamoss, the Leaf Rider, stroked Frisbee. The cat lay down and the Leaf Rider climbed aboard.

Dubber said, "I told you he was gentle. Isn't beast riding great?"

Dubber walked ahead leading the cat along the shore.

"This has many possibilities, Dubber," Seamoss said. He looked around him interested in the view from the cat's neck.

Dubber said, "We have adventures outside our own territories. We explore the park, but you know about the park. You come to the room of the Presage and see the game we play there. All of the Leaf Riders are invited."

"Have you seen the boat of the Presage?" Seamoss asked. "That is what I want more than anything, the Presage's boat. I want it for myself. Could you get it for me?"

"You want to own something you did not find yourself?" Dubber said. "I can't transfer that boat to you! That is not done! I can't take the Presage's boat. It is not mine. It is not even a natural thing, it is something that the Presage made. We gather things from the places we live, we do not take things from somewhere else. I can show you the video game because we only use it in the Presage's room. He lets us use it, we don't move it, or take it outside."

Dubber studied Seamoss a minute.

Seamoss said, "I want to go fast. I want to be the best Leaf Rider in my clan. That boat will help me do it. So I found it in the Presage's hand, I still found it didn't I?"

"There is nothing else you want? What about learning to play video games? I don't know about getting the boat, the Presage is very careful with it. He wants to win his race during their summer games," Dubber said.

Seamoss demanded, "I want that boat! Video games are of no use to me. We can teach you to swim, or leaf ride if you want, but I want the boat. I'll only bargain for the boat."

"Let me think about it. Getting the boat is very serious," Dubber said. He led the cat back. "Are you sure there is nothing else you want?"

"It's the boat or nothing," Seamoss said.

When she met me on the path, Angela said, "I can't wait to win the championship game." She pulled on her cap and we headed across the park to the ball field.

"I can wait," I said. "I watch Stanley with his crazy behavior as he acts nuttso. He hasn't eaten anything but chicken legs and spinach for a week. His brothers are complaining about the menu, but Stanley wants lucky food."

"Why chicken legs and spinach?" Angela asked.

"Don't know. He also hasn't washed his socks, or his lucky shirt for a week. He's starting to smell. He wants everyone on the team to eat like he does. He is getting his superstitions from the internet! He wants a guaranteed win."

"Chicken legs...ugh...I'm washing my shirt and my socks," Angela said. She smelled like a spring fresh fabric softner.

"Me, too."

"Look, there's Ted," Angela pointed to the distant figure coming behind us toward the ball field.

Ted sat on the bench beside me.

"Never imagined you would make it this far," he said.

"Me either," I agreed.

"Are the girls winners?" he asked.

"Obviously, there's a bunch of good ballplayers here. You don't notice they're girls when you're on the field with them. What are you doing this summer?" I asked.

"I've been taking music lessons. Piano. I like it a lot and I'm good at it. Finally something I can do. I came to watch you play, cheer even," Ted said.

"Glad to have you cheering," I said. Angela approached the bench. "See how far you can go with girls on your team?" she asked.

"I'm sorry. I hope we can still be friends," Ted said. She studied his face for a moment.

"Of course, we can be friends," she said.

Angela and I played video games with Dubber and his crew one rainy afternoon between the ball game and the boat races. We beat the little crew but their efforts and their determination made them fierce competition. Dubber skated on the mouse pad as fast as he could, and Raddit and Fluw worked the arrow keys with such precision that they almost succeeded in beating us.

"I want to be champion of this room and the Dust Bunny Punwees," Dubber said. He stood defiantly after the victory escaped him. He studied Anglea and smiled.

"Angela beat us again. Maybe it is her destiny to always win. Will you win at the boat races?" he asked.

"I'm going for it," Angela said. "I can at least beat Striper." She picked my boat off the shelf and studied the bottom of it before setting it beside Dubber.

"This is Presage's boat?" he asked. He moved to stand beside the craft when Angela returned it to the shelf.

"Yes, that is my boat. I hope to beat Angela's Scarlet, not looking too good," I said.

"Is the boat very fast?" Dubber asked.

"I think it is, not proven, yet. I keep practicing my release and hoping just like you do when you are playing games. Practicing and hoping," I said.

"Today is our game day here. Let's play again," Dubber said. He positioned himself on the mouse pad so that he was ready to start.

CHAPTER EIGHT

"I'm ready to swim," Dubber said as he slid from Frisbee and marched along the sand. Seamoss stood alone waiting.

"I will teach you, and you will bring the striped vessel to me." Seamoss turned and waded into the water. Dubber followed. He splashed sputtering as he tried to master the movements. Finally he climbed out of the water next to Seamoss.

"My first lesson," Dubber said. He dripped as he headed back to Frisbee. "I must get home before the others miss me. They'll have questions." He climbed aboard Frisbee waving goodbye to the Leaf Rider.

"Where have you been?" Raddit demanded. Fluw stood beside him. They waited on the floor beneath the video game. "We're going to practice this morning."

"I went to the pond for my first swimming lesson. Are you going to swim?" He looked from one face to the other.

"How could you leave the room without us? We thought we were in a team," Raddit said.

"Are you going to learn to swim?" Dubber repeated. The other Punwees shifted their weight on their feet.

"I don't want to swim. I don't want to be wet," Fluw said.

"You, too?" he asked Raddit. He pointed his hand in his direction.

"Yes. Are you safe going alone?" Fluw asked.

Dubber said, "Are you happy with the size of this room. You know there is a big world waiting for us to explore? Video games are just a start."

Dubber's determination to learn to swim led him to repeat visits on the beach. One day Dubber asked, "Can I swim enough to have a ride on one of your leaves?"

Seamoss studied him. "Okay, but you ride in secret. I don't want the other riders to know that I'm sharing this skill with another clan. We must do this at sunrise."

Dubber said, "Okay, I just want to ride."

The sun rose and Dubber shivered on the beach huddled into Frisbee's fur.

Seamoss greeted him and they hiked up to the leaf release point. Seamoss gestured to a modified oak leaf that lay on the beach. "This is our ride, you must sit in the front and use these handholds while I steer." He indicated the woven ropes attached to the side of the leaf. They pushed the leaf into the dropping water and Dubber struggled aboard. He grabbed the handholds and gripped them tightly. As he settled into the middle of the leaf along the central vein, Seamoss moved gracefully on the rear of the leaf to steer it around the obstacles before them. As the leaf increased in speed, Dubber made himself smaller. Seamoss moved confidently from side to side as he stood and steered the leaf out into the basin of the pond.

Seamoss asked, "What do you think?"

"Exciting, not like anything I've done before. Do you think I could be a Leaf Rider?" Dubber asked.

"We train from the time we are tiny, I don't think you could ever be good enough. My father and grandfather were leaf riders," Seamoss said.

"That's disappointing," Dubber said.

Seamoss said, "You are one of the few people outside our clan who has ever had a ride. You should be happy with that."

Dubber stood silently for a moment. He returned to the beach and called to Frisbee.

I sat on the bench waiting for the championship game to start when I heard the music getting louder. Soon Ted stood beside the bench with his music blaring.

"Listen to the theme song I picked for the team," he demanded.

"We are winners…it's what we do…"

Ted asked, "What do you think?"

The players looked around for the sound.

"What is going on?" Angela asked. She walked up to inspect.

"I've selected this as the team's theme song. You don't have a theme song, do you?" The other players moved closer forming a circle around us.

Ted said, "I'll play this whenever you take the field."

The girls cheered and pounded Ted on the back.

"Our music mascot. Hooray!" they shouted.

No one stood next to Stanley in the huddles or sat next to him on the bench.

"Stanley your stinking shirt and socks will not win the game. Don't think the chicken legs or the spinach help you either," Angela said. The team rushed out onto the field and played the game with the joy of experienced ball players. They knew what they were doing. When the ninth inning was over, the team sprayed the sticky purple sports drink around and cheered. They bowed to each other.

The theme song blared and the First Block Irregulars didn't have a chance against us. They played well and defeated the many teams from the neighborhoods around Blytheville but they were up against the precision infield and the eagle-eyed outfield. Making the play was the business of our team.

Stanley yelled, "Mason, thank you! Team thank you for your playing!"

"You're fitting in! I told you we could do it," Angela said as we walked home. I pulled the wagon of equipment and left over drinks.

I answered, "Yes, thanks for your help. Might start the fifth grade as a normal person after all, and I'm not even good at baseball."

CHAPTER NINE

Using his climbing rope with the grappling hook, Dubber climbed up the shelves to where the striped boat lay. He wound the rope around both ends and slowly lowered it onto the ground. Daylight was just breaking through the windows and Mason slept innocently in his bed. Lowering the boat on the floor, Dubber called Frisbee to him. He tied the vessel close to Frisbee's chest behind his front legs where it wouldn't be seen. Frisbee stood quietly for all of this and Dubber climbed onto his back for their trip down the stairs. Silently they slipped through the pet door and moved in the soft light toward the beach where Seamoss waited.

Creeping along in the soft dawn light, Frisbee moved onto the shore where Seamoss stood. They untied the craft from the cat. Seamoss dragged it to the pond reeds, tied it up, and hid it.

Dubber asked, "Will this get me more lessons? I want to know how to ride the leaves."

"Many more lessons," Seamoss said.

"What will you do with the boat? It's a secret that you have it," Dubber said.

Seamoss answered, "I'll practice my rides so that I can win the Leaf Rider races."

"Good luck." Dubber climbed up on Frisbee and they went back to Mason's room.

Shonar, Danu, and Phylla crept along the reeds following Seamoss in the early morning light. They suspected something when he began to retire early in the evening and delay his morning practices. They watched him move the striped craft from its hiding spot and paddle it against the current to the place where their rides began. Seamoss pulled the craft ashore before reentering the water for the ride downstream. As they watched him, Danu observed: "This thing is faster than any leaf we have found. It is hard and must be different to steer, but look at him. We can never hope to beat him in that thing."

Shonar said, "He is riding in it without a partner. It takes two of us to steer a leaf. How is he doing that and where did he learn new ways of riding? Is he going to race without a partner?"

Danu said, "How can he eliminate a partner? We have been partners from birth, this is not right. It goes against everything the team of Leaf Riders stands for."

"We're going to talk to him. Who does he think he is that he can get away without his partner. He violates the tradition of teams, the code of the Leaf Riders," Shonar said.

They watched Seamoss ride, practice his entry, and hide his boat in the reeds. As he walked along the beach path, they startled him when they stepped out and surrounded him.

Shonar asked, "Where have you been? We have watched you in the water with your strange craft."

Seamoss shifted in the middle of the circle, not meeting their gaze.

"Well..." Shonar continued.

"I want to win the Leaf Rider race," Seamoss said. He stared defiantly into each face. "I want to be the best and with this boat, I can beat all of you. Alone, by myself, I can have all the glory and become supreme champion."

Danu said, "This boat gives you an unfair advantage. We want our own boats. We'll have one."

"I have the only one. This is the Presage's boat. He doesn't know I have it. Dubber brought it to me in exchange for leaf riding, and swimming skills."

Shonar gasped, "You are teaching our secrets to outsiders."

Seamoss hung his head.

Danu spoke, "You'll get us a vessel." Her words had a final ring to them.

"How?" Seamoss asked.

"You will find a way for us to have our own boat and then we'll race on rider skills," Shonar said.

"I'll have to think about this," Seamoss said as they started up the slope to their homes.

CHAPTER TEN

In the excitement and preparations of the championship baseball game, I didn't miss my striped boat. The day of the race, I woke up and discovered it wasn't in its place on my shelf.

"I'm cleaning my room, looking for some of my stuff. I have things missing." I called to my mom as I pulled the vacuum out of the hall closet.

My mom said, "It's about time. The dust bunnies are taking over. I know you have been busy but it's time to be clean. I'm still finding your computer on in the mornings after you've gone out."

I vacuum, dusted, and mopped. I picked up everything in the room, and hung up my clothes. I moved my furniture, but no striped boat. I was too busy to notice that the Dust Bunny Punwees were nowhere to be found.

I called Angela to help me look.

Angela said, "It has to be here somewhere. I want to beat you fair and square. It's not right to have the boat go missing before the race."

"I've looked everywhere. My mom hasn't been in my room, she left the cleaning to me so she didn't move it. I don't know where to look next."

Shonar, Danu, Phylla, and Seamoss waded in the reeds where the striped boat was tied.

"It's shallow here. Maybe when the boats are released for the race, we can secure them," Shonar said.

"What if we create a net out of the water reeds growing in the pond along the banks? We can use that net to capture them. We only need a minute to climb aboard. We can cut the net and then race into the middle," Danu said.

Phylla said, "That's a good idea. We only need to slow the vessels down so we can climb on. We don't need to make them stand still. We're Leaf Riders."

"That might work. Slow the boats down, board them, and take control of the ride," Seamoss said. They gathered and dried the pond weeds. They wove the fibers into tiny ropes and connected them to make nets. They had a net long enough to stretch across the water opening after the boats rushed down from the rapids. They secured their net under the surface of the water where it couldn't be seen.

Seamoss said, "They will be coming down this stretch of water very fast. Can everyone board? We can stand on the nets just below the water, but we'll have to scramble to get on the boats. I can pull the striped vessel from the reeds, float out, and help."

Danu said, "We are good climbers. We can climb aboard the boats then we will see who is the best rider. The current will help us get back into the middle."

Stanley, Ted, Angela, and two others stood at the release point ready to drop their boats into the currents rushing down from the culvert.

"Get ready, steady, drop your boats now," the announcer shouted. The boats entered the stream and sailed along.

"Go, Scarlet, Go," Angela shouted as she walked along the bank. "Come on!"

The boats rushed down the stream. Then they hung where the stream met the pond. Suspended for an instant. I watched as flashes of light moved from the water to the inside of the vessels.

"What is going on! Angela called.

Stanley said, "It looks like they hung on something."

I saw my striped boat dart from the reeds into the main current. Seamoss steered toward the other boats and then turned his craft into the current. He took the lead. The others settled into their positions and rushed into the currents. Seamoss still led.

Angela called, "There goes Striper. I thought you'd lost it. What's it doing in the water?" I shrugged.

The riders moved into the center of the pond still fighting for the lead, they piled-up, a snarl of small boats careening in all directions. Striper spun off into the side of the scarlet boat. I watched two of the Leaf Riders as they were thrown from their boats. They sank into the swirling foam as the vessels slamming together churned the water. Seamoss emerged from the bottom of Striper and steered his way to lead. Angela's Scarlet closed in behind him as Shonar took control of it. Stanley's boat spun out of the current and moved to the shoreline with the waves. Ted's boat shattered in the collision. The pieces were covered with the water and sank out of sight. The other two boats cleared the current and drifted off course, no longer part of the race.

I watched my striped boat race toward the waterfall at a breakneck speed. Seamoss lost control as the boat lifted, clearing the dam, and crashing on the rocks used for flood control. Shonar brought Scarlet to the bank. He reentered the water and moved back to the original boat crash looking for Danu and Phylla. I could see his head bob as he came up for breath. I couldn't locate Danu and Phylla.

I waded into the pond looking for signs of the tiny Leaf Riders. As I scooped the water up and scanned it, Stanley called from the bank, "What are you doing? What are you looking for?"

"Nothing, as the water ran through my hands. Nothing," I answered.

CHAPTER ELEVEN

Angela sat beside me. I dripped water and held my head. She held the fragments of both boats in her hands.

Angela held it out. "I have what's left of your boat."

I couldn't look at it.

"Seamoss, Danu, and Phylla are not here," I whispered. "They haven't been found." I took the boat fragments studying them for clues.

"It's time for the picnic. Your parents will be waiting for you," Angela said.

I watched as teams of leaf bearers pulled the missing Punwees from along the shore where they had drifted. Tiny soggy masses without their sparkle lay limp as they were carried along. Seamoss ran up and down the beach encouraging the searchers as they recovered his comrades. I sat in silence hoping everything was going to be all right, but fearing the news.

Angela joined me. "Are they going to be alright?"

"Don't know. They are not talking to me right now. Can you blame them?" I asked.

"How were you to know they would steal your boat and wreck it?" Angela asked.

"It was exciting to see them ride their leaves. I didn't imagine they would want to do more than that," I answered.

"How did they get your boat?" Angela asked.

"I'll have to ask questions. Don't know how," I answered.

When we arrived at the picnic table, my parents waited for us.

My Dad said, "Just heard about the boat wreck."

"I don't think making boats and winning races is my thing either. Not baseball, not small boat building," I said.

"You'll figure it out," Dad said.

There was silence in my room. Absent were the skater, and the arrow key workers. Dubber, Raddit, and Fluw didn't show themselves. Frisbee slept on my bed quiet and still.

Angela said, "My friends are still talking about the wreck at the races. Not sure wading in the pond and shouting: 'No! No! It can't be!' helped your campaign to be normal. There were kids from the fifth grade watching."

"I was lost in the excitement. My boat appeared out of nowhere. How did it get there?" I asked.

"The place to start looking is among the Punwees we haven't seen today. How did they move it off your shelf," Angela said.

"And when. While I was busy with the championship game, I guess. I didn't miss it the day it moved."

"They are tiny, the boat is much bigger than they are. Do you think it took the three of them?" Angela asked.

"Can't imagine how they did it. Since they have disappeared, I guess I'll have to go to the Council Rose and to talk to someone."

I sat next to the Council Rose and called to Tolemar, the Miniscule. "Tolemar, I need to meet with the Council. I am your Presage, I need to talk to you."

Silence answered me.

"They didn't answer me when I called to them," I said. Angela and I were sitting in my room getting ready to play.

Angela said, "I've missed their enthusiasm and competition."

"Are you saying that I'm no fun?" I asked.

"You're predictable," she answered. "They added an element of surprise, maybe cause I can't see them."

CHAPTER TWELVE

I made it part of my routine to sit beside the Council Rose for an hour every morning. School would start soon and I needed to get my answers.

While I waited one morning, I heard shouts. Kids that I did not know played a game in the park. As I sat on the slope leading down into the park there were some in red shirts and some just wore their colored t-shirts.

I watched as they clustered down below and all of them grabbed a colored tennis ball from the covered bucket that they moved into their center. Some balls were red and some were yellow. The bucket remained where it was as they scattered around the park hiding. One by one they slipped from their hiding place and rushed to the bucket where they dropped their ball. The red shirts then tried to block the other players from reaching the bucket by chasing them. If they succeeded in capturing them, they took their ball and swapped it for a red one. The players charged the bucket and sometimes they were intercepted by one of the others.

"What are they trying to do?" I studied the scene trying to make sense of the activity. Angela joined me on my third morning while I waited beside the rose bush.

"We're going to have to ask them. It looks like some kind of tag," Angela said.

"I don't know any of these kids. Where are they from?" I asked.

"Never seen them before, I'm new here too," Angela said.

We rose and moved down closer to the bucket.

"Let's ask," Angela said.

"What're you playing?" I called.

Twins popped up from behind a bush and called, "American Revolution, the Battle of Lexington."

"How do you play?" I asked.

"Pick a side, Redcoats or Colonists. Redcoats wear the red t-shirts. Then you try to capture their ammo, the tennis ball before they can get it into the bucket. If they get it into the bucket, then they are safe. The side with the most balls in the bucket wins."

My name is Brad and his name is Charlie. He is my brother," Brad said.

Charlie called, "We the twins. We live on Adams and everyone meets in the parks in the mornings to play our game, 'American Revolution.'

"How many are you? Why haven't we seen you before?" Angela asked.

"We are only here in the mornings, that's the only time we can play," Brad said.

"Come in everyone and meet the new kids. Maybe they will play with us?" Charlie called out. He waved his hands signaling a time out.

They gathered from everywhere. Some of them had sticks and leaves in their hair as they stepped from their hiding places and moved to where we stood. There were three colonists and three Redcoats. As they introduced themselves, they told what grade they were in. Two of them were older, sixth graders, Mike and Ben, one was a fifth grader, Greg. Blake, Greg's third grade brother, played. The twins were fourth graders.

"I didn't know there were so many kids living around this park," I said. Angela nodded her head in agreement.

"During school we only play on Saturday mornings, but it is summer, and we play every day we can," Charlie said.

They all nodded their heads in agreement.

"School starts and we don't have time to be in the park. Homework, ugh," Charlie said.

"Summer is for 'American Revolution'," Brad said.

"Hooray!" they all cheered.

"Come play with us. Here is a tennis ball, wear a red shirt next time if you want to be a Redcoat. Today you have to be a colonist."

Charlie explained, "We are from the Third Street side of the park. We've just moved the game from that side to this side. We wanted different."

Brad said, "Everyone knew where to hide on that side so we brought the game here for new territory."

Ben said, "We've been playing this game in the park for two summers now. Sometimes we build a bonfire in the firepit and sit around and talk about the game while we roast marshmallows."

Mike said, "Parents encourage us to be outside and run around getting exercise."

Greg said, "It gets us out of the house and we all watch my brother Blake and keep him out of trouble."

Ben said, "When we were in the fourth grade our history lesson was about Paul Revere's ride and the battle of Lexington."

Angela and I took our tennis ball and joined the 'American Revolution.'

As we were leaving, Angela said, "That was fun! Got my exercise for the day."

"More going on in the neighborhood and park than I imagined. We'll have to join more often," I said.

Finally Tolemar appeared.

"The Council will convene this evening. We will meet with you then." Tolemar said.

"I'll be here."

The light of the sun dimmed across the park as the shadows of the trees closed in around the bowl shape. The last rays of the sun shone on the roses as I waited. Finally they gathered. Tolemar stood with the clan gathering behind him. He strode to stand in front of me.

He began, "We have findings to report. The exchange of our cultures has not benefited us. Our youth have learned to crave things that are not in our traditions. Traditions that have helped us survive for many generations. We never interact with your culture. We live quietly and simply. Shonar, Danu, and Phylla were injured by the rides too advanced for them. Seamoss has supplied details of how the boats were secured. He made Dubber get the striped boat for him in exchange for swimming lessons and leaf rides. This interaction among the clans is without example in our history. We have never intermingled our knowledge in this manner. Each clan keeps to themselves and does not share ideas with other clans in this way.

Dubber removed from you the boat that did not belong to him with the aid of the cat. He delivered it to the Leaf Rider, Seamoss. When the other Leaf Rider saw it, they conspired to take the rest of the boats. The boats are something that it is not natural for them. They don't have the skills to control them. Video games are not natural for them. We conclude there is no benefit for our clans to have these skills.

Therefore, we will disappear from your sight. We will relocate to a place where no one can see us. It is for our own protection. We will insure that our youth do not explore outside their established boundries. From this day forth you will not see us, we will not talk to you, the Dust Bunnies have already selected a new location where they are not seen. We no longer need you as our Presage. You will never see us again."

I sat and watched them fade into the Council Rose and the surrounding grass.

As I walked home, I listed in my mind the benefits of never seeing them again, and the things I would miss. They were entertaining, and we did have adventures as I tried to adjust to this new location where Dad moved us. I imagine there are many things in the world that I've never noticed. The Punwees were just one example.

Angela asked, "They're gone? Will never see or hear them again? They won't play video games? You're just like the rest of us?"

I said, "Yes, that's the size of it. They're gone. Mom even thinks my room is cleaner cause she hasn't seen a dust bunny around my baseboards."

Stanley joined us in my room in the afternoons.

Stanley said, "Going to miss baseball. Let's play video games again. School starts soon."

www.ingramcontent.com/pod-product-compliance
Lightning Source LLC
LaVergne TN
LVHW020426080526
838202LV00055B/5048